One More Number

One More Number

Craig Rodgers

Death of Print

ISBN: 9781087990880

deathofprint.press

"The Trumpet Man" was first published in *Not One of Us* #59, April 2018. "He Is in a Clearing If You Can Find It" was first published in *HAD*, September 2020. "Our Featured Performer" was first published in *Chicago Literati* in 2017 or 2018 and republished in *Moonchild Magazine* in 2019.

The font used for the main text is STIXGeneral. The old-time movie font is Good Bad Man, designed by Chank Diesel. "Musical Symbol Silhouette" created by Piotr Siedlecki.

The Trumpet Man

1

In the end Silas takes nothing. He stares at the box they give him and the years of detritus accumulated on his desk, papers and baubles and photos of memories not worth remembering, and he leaves it all. They tell him to clean out his desk, to take his things and go, but as he stands looking at the gathered decorations of his pocket universe these items become unrecognizable—evidences of someone else's life.

Faces linger in the doorway, refugees from another department come to fill a moment with the detached humiliation of a stranger. They talk in whispers and ogle without shame. A phone ringing somewhere pulls them away from the spectacle. Someone from Human Resources comes by to speak with Silas but he has already gone.

Each light is green. They start red and they change or they're fixed on go as Silas is propelled onward unobstructed through beckoning streets, away from one world and nearer another, a destination conceived but unknown, the idea of a place. Unformed, all potential.

Children play in snow still falling. They turn their faces up and blink back ice tears. They laugh in the cold, every breath a cloud. A man scrapes snow from a windshield. Shopkeepers shovel sidewalks. Silas drives between their worlds as a song plays on the radio. He sings along with the parts he knows.

He comes in to buy a drink but instead he orders coffee. The server asks him what kind and he doesn't know. Coffee.

A man eats from a plate, not his, something left behind by a diner now gone. Fine tailored suit, fabric dark, loose. The man laughs at a story he himself tells as a waitress nods along. Bread soaks up grease and he talks as he chews.

The coffee arrives and Silas sips. It's black and it's bitter. He looks for sugar but there is none. Silas drinks the coffee black. The waitress laughs and she nods and the man in the fine suit lets her slip away from his charms.

Drink orders replace food orders as the day crowd creeps away, supplanted by something else; youths with faces pink from cold come in for drink or just to warm, drinkers there for no reason but that, unbound revelers flinging shouts across the gathered forms of strangers to some other hidden face on the room's far side, narrow-eyed wanderers observing the world in silence, all manner of person. Citizens now freed from day.

A raised dais occupies one wall. A place for musical instruments but there are none here. Cords connect to nothing, snake off to nowhere. A single stand sits empty of microphone. A bartender with a wild mustache points at that place and speaks with a woman, the bar owner, someone quiet who waits and nods and doesn't speak, only listens, the bartender's words making their way to her but falling short of Silas, who bends across the bar but catches not enough to understand. The owner turns. She stares.

"Can I get a drink?" asks Silas.

The owner leans and she speaks to the bartender and he nods and she turns and moves through a door behind the bar. Silas selects something from a line of names on a chalkboard. The drink arrives and he sips and it is iced and then warm and sweet. He sips again.

There is music, a song growing out of the electric hiss of countless bodies talking at once, a speaker someplace swelling with the noise it contains until a tune can be heard above that human chorus. A man moves through the gathered revelers. He wears a dark sweater, he carries a case. Stubble lines skull, shaved days ago, a week ago. He orders a drink with no ice and he sets the case on the bar. The thrum of popping latches. A trumpet is set among newspaper yellowed with age. Pouches and pockets line the walls. He digs through several until he finds what he's looking for. Coins plunk down onto the counter, currency smeared with grime, with oil, each stamped with the face of some strange, forgotten man or other.

The bartender looks at the coins and he looks at the man. He pours the drink and when the man reaches for it he leans forward to speak. Words are swallowed by a room unconcerned with the fleeting secrets shared by this moment or any. The man listens, the bartender speaks. After long moments the man nods. Silas watches, immersed in the idea of all that might be said. He speaks up only after the bartender is gone.

"What was that?"

The trumpet man blinks and he turns to Silas.

"He said another drink will cost me a song."

"Okay."

"Fuck him."

"Fuck him?"

"He doesn't know the value of things."

"Seems like a bargain."

"You don't know the value of things."

Silas snorts.

"Okay."

The trumpet man stares, waits. He stands and he pushes his way through the mass of writhing bodies. A table in one corner is scratched with the pedestrian musings of guests long past. The trumpet man sits with his drink and his case and the swath he cut through the room is swallowed up by the swaying organism the gathered create.

The man in the fine suit watches these moments from his place at bar's end. He waves a hand and the waitress brings a drink. He whispers and she laughs and brings another. He points at the distant figure of the trumpet man. *And the same for my friend*, he tells her. He says it dry, maybe sincere, maybe not.

The drink arrives at the table and the trumpet man tenses. He speaks and the waitress shrugs and he stands. He returns to the bar. The bartender is there waiting. They talk and then they talk louder. People are turning. Some laugh. The trumpet man shakes with anger. He points at the bartender and he's shouting now. The owner steps back into the room. An electronic cigarette hangs from her hand. She touches the stem to her lips and she breathes. The man in the fine suit smiles his smile and he trades words with the owner. She laughs, a bawdy guffaw in the silence left in the wake of the shouting. A cloud swirls around the circle of her face. The room waits as seconds pass. A man steps forward and then another. Red of face, visibly drunk. One touches the arm of the trumpet man, but the trumpet man balks, he spins. He is ready to fight but they are on him and he is being dragged to the door, into the night. The crowd cheers.

Silas moves through the room, not watching as the mob dissolves and the music returns, no one quite sure when it stopped. He takes a seat at the scarred bar table. The case is there with a drink untouched.

There is a rhythm to the noise of a thousand drunk bodies at once let loose on the night, from this bar, from the next one, the one after that, a swelling of steps and of voices followed by a gradual falling off. Left behind are the stragglers and the crunch of ice underfoot as they drift in ones and twos off into the dark.

Silas is there, a fixed point in the flow until there is only him. He sways on his feet and when the wind picks up he pulls his coat close around him, cloth bunched in one fist, the other arm drooping with the weight of the case. Cold grows. Silas shivers, he closes his eyes.

A thump and then the indefinable noise of movement somewhere, not here. A man in a fine suit rounds the corner of the building and is there, is standing. He holds an electric cigarette that he puts to his mouth and inhales, holds. He tosses the trinket into the night. Thud and bounce and gone. Smoke leaks with words.

"Are you lost?"

Silas shakes his head.

"Just taking a moment. Are you?"

"Lost?'

"Yeah."

The man in the fine suit stands staring, words unformed, mouth ajar. He points at nothing in particular.

"No. I'm going this way."

He turns and he walks into the street. He doesn't look back and soon he is gone, footprints in snow leading off, away from the light.

Silas finds his car. Hours of snowdrift surround. He climbs in and he turns the key and a song is playing on the radio. He listens, at times he hums along. He closes his eyes and tilts the seat back.

The cold has gotten in. The heater is off. The car is off. Silas blinks and he breathes and one hand turns the key. The sounds don't come, the spark and hum of engine life, the click of hope, the radio, the heater.

Something is burning. Snow cakes the windshield and the world is gone. Silas steps out of the car and he's unsteady. Still drunk, still half asleep. Streetlights find smoke up the block. Silas turns and with the trumpet case walks the other direction along the trail where footprints had been but now are not. Somewhere a siren begins to wail.

Every head is turned away. Televisions display the same news anchor standing in front of the same map, pointing, speaking. Reds and yellows wash across the depicted landscape, a projection of calamity. Cut to a shot of white, miles of thick snow broken only by four lanes of unmoving cars, headlights illuminating splashes of static night. A hundred cars or a thousand, ten thousand.

The man at the counter is slow to turn. Silas steps up and speaks and the man's face moves but his eyes remain fixed on the television screen for another second, two seconds, before meeting the man that stands before him.

"Do you have a payphone?"

The counterman scoffs.

"Come on," he says.

"What?"

"Nobody has a payphone."

Silas looks around the room.

"I just need a cab."

The counterman tilts his head. Swelling disdain lines his features.

"There's a blizzard."

Silas opens his mouth but no retort comes. The counterman returns his attention to the flickering screen and its prophet now declaiming fated woe. Ominous splotches spread across the world. The weatherman's tie is crooked.

Most seats are empty, a few occupied by the post-bar wanderers or those caught out in the snow. Silas takes a paper menu and a chair. He runs a finger down lines of items, familiar dishes with colorful names, witty descriptions. He orders and he eats and for some time the only sound is the television and now and then from some turned-away face a whispered testimony to the horror of it all.

A man takes the seat across from Silas. He wears a heavy coat from which he pulls one gloved hand to point at the case waiting next to Silas.

"Did you steal that?"

Silas shrugs. The man is still talking.

"I've seen the guy it belongs to. In here, around."

"He left it in a bar."

"You know him?"

"Do you?"

The man in the heavy coat shakes his head. He takes a drink from a flask when he thinks no one is looking. Wind rises and the world hums. The television goes on pronouncing doom. The weatherman on the screen is replaced once more by the image of traffic mired in white. Lights flicker but do not go out. Night screams through the open diner door and is cut off again. A man in a fine suit knocks snow from shoes. He doesn't recognize Silas, or if he does it does not show. The man in the heavy coat is speaking.

"They're shutting down the highway."

Stunned faces look out through car windows. Some step out into frigid night. A reporter moves along asking questions that no one can answer. She points a microphone at an older man standing in the open door of an idling sedan. A bell is pinging, the radio is on. The reporter asks the older man what he is going to do now but he says he does not know.

They gather in the church up the block and in the shelter beyond that. Lights in windows mark sanctuary. Offices, shops. Anyplace that will have them.

Silas moves through these few blocks, looking in at the faces of strangers huddled in each place.

They look out at the storm and the world or they look at each other with wide eyes, glazed eyes, stricken by the enormity of a thing they cannot understand. Silas moves on.

The sanitizing glare of fluorescents penetrates. Supermarket, mega store, a little of everything. Castaways fill the aisles. Silas enters in a wash of heat from bodies and breath and a boiler pumping warmth into the vast warehouse of diverse consumables. No one mans the checkouts, no nametags or uniforms are present. Cameras overhead record the world but if someone is watching they do not appear. Shelves once stacked with breads now stand bare. Coolers are picked clean of milk, of juices, pizzas, meals for one. Water is gone. No one at hand has bread or milk. Whatever happened was over when these strays found their way to this place. Some sleep in chairs on display, some use their own clothes as pillows balled in knots. The lucky ones found stuffed animals, toys soft, inviting, a place to lay a tired head. Silas moves among bodies sprawled, faces turned up to see what passes their way. Not finding what he's come for, he leaves.

Blocks and cold. Dawn is still hours off. The streets are free of life. Only the wind moves here. Silas squints and he tucks his head but the storm is unrelenting. He moves in the direction of noise, of light.

The church is filled when Silas enters. People shiver and stomp feet to get the cold out or they huddle together and share their warmth. Some blink and stare. Heaters moan, coils glowing in their open mouths. Talk goes on in pockets, a hundred conversations running together. Voices carry and blend with the wind, a medley, a chorus in the night. Someone produces a bottle hidden away and this they pass around and soon there is another one following much the same route. Somewhere there is laughter. The wind grows and it howls and there is a creaking in the walls, a groan of old wood. Silas searches the faces but the trumpet man is not one of them.

A priest is moving among the huddled congregation. He talks or he listens. He asks questions; about their lives, how they're holding together, small things, big things. He comforts them. He touches a hand or he nods when needed. A woman sits in one corner making no sound as she sobs and in another a man taps at a phone. A radio plays a song or maybe that too is a phone. The restless settle and there is a peace that blooms. Silas speaks to no one and after several minutes he leaves by the same doors through which he entered that holy place.

Snow falls and is dragged across ground thick with accumulation. Silas stands on the church stoop looking out at the falling white and a wind that follows an impulse capricious or mad. He is not alone. The man in the fine suit seems not to notice the wind, the snow, the bite of the world. He is draped in a heavy coat that he did not wear before.

"Not for you, huh?"

"What?" says Silas.

The man in the fine suit hooks a thumb at the doors at his back and the worlds they contain.

"I was looking for someone."

The man in the fine suit pauses to consider this. He looks at Silas and at the street. Sound comes from inside the church but it is a dull hum, a thing without form, meaningless here. The man speaks.

"Drink?"

Silas puts up a hand with pale fingers splayed. No. The man takes a flask from a coat pocket and unscrews the spout. He gestures at the street and the storm and the world.

"You see this?"

And.

"Some weather."

He laughs as he says it and he pours a colorless broth into his maw. Silas responds but his words are lost, in the wind, in the night, more. There is a siren. It screams, a portent at first and then more, a physical thing beating the senses over and over, growing, now felt, now heard, gripping, wringing, eating all sound, leaving behind only its own.

A fire truck passes by in the snowy street, its form and its noise there and gone, broken loose and whirling away. The man in the fine suit is speaking but the fading siren call obscures his words. He repeats himself, his name, Al.

"Albert?" says Silas. "Alphonse?"

"Aldous Begler. You?"

"Silas."

"That's an old name."

"I've had it for years."

The man doesn't laugh and maybe he doesn't hear. He takes another drink and he watches snow heaved by on a wind that vibrates the world, a hum within, soul raked and trembling. He's an insurer, he says, and maybe he is. He points out buildings and he rattles off numbers, policies held, wagers set against a desolation that is already here.

"In this storm? Someone's gonna get rich," he says. "Somebody else is fucked."

There is a pop, a sound distant but rich of nameless cataclysm that a moment later lets itself be known as the world falls piece by piece into darkness. Voices raise in a chorus of gasps, in the church, elsewhere, then fall away leaving only the wind and its sorrow sung on timeless breath. Some time later Silas feels more than sees that he is standing on the stoop alone. He steps into the street.

#

His coat lets in cold where he's lost a button. He holds it closed with fingers that ache, trumpet case in other hand, sleeve pulled low. He changes hands but it makes no difference. A man on a corner offers to sell him gloves but Silas cannot find his wallet. He checks every pocket and then he checks each one again. The man laughs like this is some private joke, a routine they've worked out together, practiced each day. He gives Silas the gloves and he asks no payment.

He tastes the smoke and then the fire is there, a glow some ways off that swells and grows wild, swinging limbs which reach up and twirl and curl in on themselves only to reform as Silas nears. A block of storefronts, once possessed of a life, now writhing and twisted with altogether something else, spouts oranges and yellows in a blackened framework, the bones of what had been now bewitched by two thousand degrees. Men garbed in the dress of their trade surround a truck from which unspools a length of hose. They loose untold gallons into the maelstrom but nothing changes. Elements blend, spinning lights atop the truck and the glimmer and call of the flames creating a show in the night, shadows moving all around. Faces appear in windows or they stream out into the snow to watch, ignorant of the cold and the snow. Silas is one of many. No one among the gathered can say just how long they watch.

There is a crash deep within of something giving way but from the outside no change shows through. Men are shouting and someone is pointing but the voices are meaningless in the roar of the fire. Some in the crowd lean in, yearning for the flames. Silas turns and walks on.

Quiet replaces chaos. Wind falls away and a stillness sets in. Snow falls straight down, loosed in a vacuum. The quiet expands. The noise of the world is not here. The animal sounds, the people sounds, honking, barking, bugs, birds. All gone now.

A woman stands in a doorway. She moves her lips but if she makes a sound Silas does not hear. He climbs steps buried by snow and she smiles and she nods and now she is speaking, now she is making sound.

"You must be so tired."

He looks at his feet and he looks at her again. Snow drifts in through the open door as the wind comes back up.

"It's okay, come in."

She takes his arm and leads him down a darkened hall. Wood floors groan. Her dress is spun wool, thick but not made for the cold. Hair tied back. She moves with confident stride through the dark like she knows the way by heart. A glow first appears and then blooms as hall leads to hall and then opens on a spare kitchen where sits a bearded man bedecked in rags leaning over an expanse of island. A single candle burns, wax rolling down to gather and grow on a plastic countertop made to look like wood.

"Stuck out in it?"

The bearded man eats from a plastic container he holds out in front of him, each distinct forkful holding something pungent, something wet. He talks between bites.

"There's a lot of that. What'd the weatherman say beforehand? Nothing. Nothing."

A siren grows and fades and another follows the first but these sounds are dulled by walls and the bearded man goes on, ignorant of these distractions. He asks Silas questions in the voice of a friend. Is he hungry? Is he tired? He is, but he gives the bearded man no answer save the continued stare of weary eyes at the trough of edible slop. The bearded man forks elegant bites into his own waiting mouth. He chews too long and he watches Silas. Sometimes he drinks from a ceramic mug, overlarge, old.

"I lost my job today," says Silas.

The bearded man laughs without mirth.

"And look at you now."

The woman leans and she whispers to the bearded man and he laughs again. She says goodnight to each man in turn and she moves into the darkness, first her form and then her footsteps disappearing into some unknown lying beyond the darkness that surrounds. The noise of the bearded man's eating is the only sound now. His face wavers in the shifting candle glow. Now he is recognizable, now he is not. Silas curls in a corner with his coat pulled around him and his head in the junction of walls, cheek unwashed and slick with cold whiskey sweat as it rests against old plaster.

The room is thick with darkness when Silas opens his eyes. He breathes and he is still alive. He stands after some time and stretches limbs that ache. Joints pop, breath hitches. He undertakes a hesitant exploration of the dark until one foot

comes in contact with the trumpet case set against
the kitchen island where it was left abandoned
some hours ago. This he hefts as he tries to
remember the way. His footsteps echo as he
stumbles to the hall and around a corner and then
another and to a door and into the violent
appearance of sunlight and morning. The sky is
white, the ground is white, a uniform brightness
that tears at the mind. His stomach churns and rolls
and he leans against a doorframe cut from a tree
now a century dead. He breathes. In time he
straightens. The cold is everywhere now.

2

The faces have all changed. Diners fork mouthfuls of egg or sausage or things drenched in syrup as they talk in exuberant pairings or huddled collectives, the survivors, the reborn. Daylight bathes the room through windows unshuttered. The weatherman is pointing at his maps on the television screen but the volume is down and no one is listening.

Aldous sits at a table with a man in an apron. The apron man drinks coffee from a mug and so does Aldous. A pot half full sits in the middle of the table. Aldous looks up as Silas enters. He points to a chair, old friends now. The coat he wears is not the one from the night before, this one thick, dark, expensive. Silas sits at the table.

"That bar burned down last night. A few hours earlier and we might've been there."

A tray of clean mugs sits on a nearby table beside an oversized jar stuffed with bills. Silas pats pockets but his wallet isn't there. Crumpled dollars are tucked in among other items of mystery in an inner pocket. He sticks a dollar in the jar's waiting mouth and takes a mug. He pours coffee and sips. The coffee is cold.

"Somebody got burned up. They're saying it's the owner but they don't know that."

"Things. Dental records."

Aldous stares unblinking.

"Dental records. A fire gets hot enough those teeth pop like popcorn. Fire cleanses. It absolves the land of sin. You ever wanna fake your own death, use fire."

"Nobody does that."

"Fake their own death? Don't be naive. Anything you can think of has been tried by somebody somewhere."

Silas doesn't laugh and Aldous doesn't blink.

"There was another fire up the street," says Silas.

Aldous nods.

"Yeah. This storm's a real mess."

He waits a beat, then speaks.

"What are you doing here?"

"Where?"

Aldous waves a hand around at the storm and the world. Silas looks at the table.

"I lost my job. I stopped in for a drink on the way home."

"Lost your job. What was your job?"

"Nothing special."

Aldous sits back, contemplates, speaks.

"I got stuck in it waiting on my lawyer."

"What kind of lawyer?"

"Mine."

And.

"Criminal defense."

"What'd you do?"

"The state charged me with insurance fraud, conspiracy, filing a false report, some others."

"What'd you do?" Silas says again.

"Nothing untoward. Nothing immoral. I helped some people."

"Yeah?"

Aldous shrugs.

"There's a law for everything now."

And.

"What now?"

"What now?"

"What will you do?"

"For work?"

"Okay."

Silas looks out at the snow.

"After this," says Aldous.

Silas doesn't answer.

"Who would you be if you weren't you?"

"I don't know what that means."

"A farmer? A teacher? Paint landscapes, sell them on the corner? Who would you be?"

"Maybe I'd learn to play the trumpet."

Aldous nods. He stares.

"Maybe you would," he says.

He turns from Silas and speaks to the man in the apron. He talks at length about all manner of thing and to Silas he says no more. Silas stands. His body aches and he does not remember the last time he ate. He looks at the cold coffee he has left behind. He looks to the counter but there is no one there and the man in the apron listens with rapt attention to all that Aldous is saying. Cutlery scrapes dishware. All around patrons eat and talk, absorbed by only this moment in time. Silas opens the door and steps into the street. The wind moans.

A loudspeaker carries shouts from somewhere blocks away but the words are muddled noise, vague barks of some command whose urgency is lost as syllables break against buildings frozen and opaque with rime. Snow drifts down, no hurry now, flakes falling and piling upon the layers built up over time to form the hills and valleys of the world, the hard lines succumbing to this new way.

Silas stands numb among the few bodies moving in this new world. Strangers bury hands in pockets or they wrap themselves in their own arms. One sad fool shovels a walk that soon fills up again. He arches to pop tired bones and returns to his futile obligation. These people. Some cough, some curse. A genderless waif wrapped thick with layered art silk and foam presses two fingers to lips and then moves them to exhale, venting steam into the day. Mock smoking. A snowman stands alone in a street where nothing moves, undisturbed by man or car or beast. A block away a car does make its slow way by, an older thing, long and steel, engine rumbling with low contempt. A siren plays on an endless loop somewhere else, not here.

She is there, a woman, a girl, hair blond and tangled, smiling as he walks by, a familiarity that is inappropriate, obscene. She points.

"I know that guy."

The trumpet case pulls at Silas, one arm hanging low. He nods at it but he knows what she means.

"Yeah. Did he sell you that?"

Silas shakes his head.

"Yeah. I didn't think he would. That's. I don't know. That's his."

Silas waits and so does she. Smiling, nodding. She holds a guitar like she's about to play a song or has only just finished. Wood, simple, scuffed in places. A sticker faded and illegible. The guitar's case is long and wide, red felt lining, shaped not like the guitar, made for something else entirely. A cigarette pack crumpled and empty is the only thing inside.

"Does he live around here?" asks Silas.

She looks at the guitar in her hands. Fingers pluck at strings with no purpose, just making noise. She looks up at Silas. She squints, she shrugs. He nods and he thanks her.

Smoke plumes over the tops of buildings but as he moves that direction he finds himself no closer to the source. One block, two blocks. Snow obscures the distance and wind stirs the world and maybe what burns is miles from this place. He walks on anyway.

The highway is much as it was on the television screen, only bigger and stark in its lingering quiet. Nothing moves here. Cars are packed in snow and no engine idles now. The scared eyes of motorists have all gone. The line of steel and fiberglass and snow goes on forever, a thing with no end and no beginning. Silence and dead miles.

Tracks go off in all directions, crisscrossing each other, impressions stomped by those that passed this way, one after another. Silas follows along a vague path that may have once been sidewalk, a rough course alongside the snaking line of cars. He sees no one. Shops stand empty, locked up, shuttered. A sign says HELP WANTED in the window of a bare storefront. Signs once lit up to be seen from miles away now wait in darkness, tall and proud sigils of vast interstate empires drained of life, hollow, cold. Tucked in among these remains sits a brick mansion, a model home generic and vulgar repurposed, born again. A display reads the names of recent inhabitants; a realtor, a dentist, a lawyer.

Machinery churns somewhere behind the mock abode. Relentless hum, a generator or a lawnmower. Silas opens the front door.

The blast of air is sauna hot, a wet slap to the senses. The door shutting behind him draws an audible gasp from the world. He pulls on his coat front to fan himself and then he sheds the coat like a skin.

The lobby was once a front room, a foyer where some family would hang their coats or drop their mail, their keys. Now it holds a desk, neat and dull, and little else. All doors are closed with windows dark but one. A jazz song plays, jaunty, familiar, old.

A dog watches Silas enter the room. Face rests on paws, laid flat, arranged under flesh flopped and pooled, only eyes moving, tracking Silas' transgression. A breed mixed, nameless, a thing of many parts and progenitors. Dog face like an old man, slake skin, jowls, eyes wet and sad. It makes a noise like a huff, like a belch, then it quiets and goes on watching.

A man sits behind a desk stacked high with bottles, papers, wrappers, cans opened and emptied. His hair is thinning. It stands in places, an expensive cut untended, going to pot. Face clean shaven. His feet are propped among the refuse, boots scuffed leather and thick soled, surplus from some army or other. Dress pants, cuffs frayed and stained by snow and salt and time. His undershirt is soiled and his dress shirt hangs from the back of a chair. If there is a jacket it is not here. He points at the throwback radio from which the tinny melody emanates.

"You like that?"

He waits a beat, eyes distant, half a grin.

"Yeah you do. They changed formats. In all this, you believe it? Used to be a rock station, something."

Silas sits in a chair wrapped in something soft and blue. He lays the trumpet case in his lap like a commuter on the way to some distant horizon, stuck here waiting on a bus or a train.

"Is this your office?" he says. "Are you a lawyer?"

The lawyer shrugs. He sinks further into his chair.

"I'm just another defender of the people."

"Yeah?"

"I am."

"For money?"

The lawyer examines first the question and then the man, alert and curious for maybe the first time in a long while.

"I do karma's good work. This office is a conduit through which right and wrong make themselves known."

"For money."

The lawyer smiles. He gestures at the trumpet case.

"You play?"

"It's not mine."

"Whose is it?"

"I don't know."

The lawyer puts out his hands.

"May I?"

Silas pushes the trumpet case across the desk with some hesitation. The satisfying snap of clasps sprung cuts through the moment. The lawyer pulls the trumpet from its nest like a treasure found, a gentle heft, a twinkle of awe.

"It's kind of beat up. How much you want for it?"

"It isn't mine."

The lawyer nods. He turns the object, eyeing every angle, all its parts. He sets the trumpet with much care in its bed of yellowed paper. He leans in and he stares at something there, some headline tucked in among the stash of old news. He smiles and he drops the lid.

"Hungry?"

He pushes a can of something across to Silas, a mad chef on the label. A can opener follows and then a spoon. Silas takes back the trumpet. He sets it at his feet and he waits a moment. The lawyer nods, polite. Silas opens the can.

The two men eat without talk and the radio fills the space with a big band number, all horns and crashes and great swooping changes and then the song ends and in its place is something slower, not at all the same, strings and mourning and empty spaces.

Silas reaches for the radio.

"Can I change this?"

He spins the dial past a dozen alien sounds. When it lands a newsman is talking, he's speaking of fire.

"This again," says the lawyer.

The newsman is listing off the names of places now gone, consumed by flame this day or the day before.

"I know him."

"Who?"

The lawyer gestures at the radio, at the story it tells.

"This firebug. This shit."

The newsman is telling of a city block engulfed as trucks respond from station after station but what they save will amount to little, the structures giving in already, burning or burned.

"That's my neighborhood," says Silas.

It's dark when he leaves. Night has congealed, a murk waded through in the absence of streetlamp hum or passing cars or the soothing presence of pedestrian wanderings. Wind speaks an arcane tongue, a beast howling mad words and nipping at every inch of bare skin. Snowfall touches flesh but is felt more than seen. Even moonlight is muted in this new world, hushed by a risen horror. Somewhere someone sings in the night, one or two or maybe more, a chorus of voices beautiful and haunting, an unseen harmony calling out and hungry.

There are thuds and grunting and cries of pain. An alley hides something awful, a nameless destruction, the ruin of who knows what.

"Hey," says Silas.

The sounds pause. A voice comes through from the dark.

"Keep walking."

Silas looks hard into the black but sees nothing, whatever violation occurred veiled wholly in the thickness of night. He hesitates and then he's moving, he's walking away.

Moon peeks through and for a moment the world is a painting, all blues and blacks and silence. A fire truck sits empty and abandoned on a sidestreet, a relic of hope. Of a snowman there are left only remains where someone took a bat to the figure, smashing to pieces the carrot nose, the coal eyes. A lump is all that is left. The clouds come in to take away the light.

The diner is dark but for one TV showing. The light is unmoving and devoid of sound. Silas enters and he curls in a corner. He holds the trumpet case to him like a ward against evil spirits that populate this new world. He blinks and he stares at the light of the television as sleep seeps in. The image shows the line of dead highway cars as one phantom light cuts among them, moving this way and that, but for what it is searching there is no way to know.

3

The man in the fine suit raises a spoon in greeting.

"Aldous," says Silas.

Aldous Begler nods as he eats from an open tin can. He speaks with mouth full.

"It's cold out."

Silas tries not to laugh but does anyway.

"I don't have any place to be."

Aldous asks and Silas answers; burned home, nowhere to go, the whole story. Aldous responds.

"You can stay at my place."

"Yeah?"

Aldous sets can and spoon on a mound of snow that might once have been a curb. He takes a pen from some inner pocket and scribbles an address on a paper scrap. Silas looks at the paper and he looks at this stranger. Aldous is looking at the trumpet case.

"You still carrying that thing around?"

Midday sun makes fire of every point, ground and sky and all, a piercing white that does not fail to cleanse the land of what has come before, night now washed away. Silas stands in a street empty of movement and noise and life. He walks and waits and walks again. Footprints follow in his wake but soon these become only vague indentions and then they vanish altogether.

Glass shatters, then nothing, a dozen seconds of unmoored alarm. Silas turns in place. Laughter and nothing and laughter again. Silas closes his eyes and listens and soon he is moving that way.

A storefront is shattered. There was once an aluminum sign but this now sits facedown on the snow-covered walk. Silas steps through a window and into a convenience store. Aisles are stripped and bare in some places and left untouched in others. Glass crunches underfoot, from the window, from items smashed. A man stands in front of an open cooler door. With one hand he moves leftovers aside while the other holds a bottle of something brown from which he takes the occasional pull. He looks over as Silas enters, examines this newcomer, goes back to his rummaging. Silas watches, he approaches, opening another section of cooler and taking hold of an off-brand drink that has so far survived.

The man with the bottle is watching Silas. He speaks but his words are nonsense, garbled and wet. He moves in and out of comprehensible talk, his points and his language both meandering and wild. He nods at the trumpet case and calls it a box. He talks like he knows the man it belongs to and he talks like he knows Silas. At times he speaks with uncomfortable familiarity. He takes deep drinks. He laughs. Silas asks a question.

"Do we know each other?"

The man smiles. He waves the bottle around at the world.

"We can be anyone now," he says.

He walks city streets in no hurry. He whistles and he watches a sky that remains unchanged for who knows how long. The snow has stopped and nothing moves, a world paused, hushed, waiting.

He checks the paper twice before he knocks. No one answers and he knocks again. He waits and he turns the knob. The front door is closed but not locked. He opens the door.

The smell of gasoline is a thick, violent thing. Silas recoils even as he moves forward. Reason is gone, there is no logic here. He is a man dashing room to room in full panic, blind. He comes to the living room.

Aldous looks up at Silas' arrival. Gas stains furniture and floor. Carpet is soaked in places. A cigarette hangs from his lip. He goes on pouring from a dented can.

"Hello," he says.

Silas steps toward him without a plan or a thought. Aldous tosses away the gas can. He raises arms, he bows up. Silas halts. Then he swings the trumpet case.

The hit connects with Aldous' face and his skull connects with the wall and he drops, conscious but not there, making noises like words. Silas looks at the man on the floor and the world soaked with gas. Silence unspools. The cigarette smolders on the floor just beyond the puddled gasoline. Carpet melts and blackens.

Mabel's Piano Bar

The piano player steps from the bus into a town he's never heard of. He turns in place, taking in his surroundings with the one eye not swollen shut. A streetlamp hums its white noise light. Buildings up and down the street are shaped in old brick. Along the back of the bus stop kiosk there is painted the simple emblem of a ship in a bottle. The piano player does another turn. The bus pulls away.

Shop windows are darkened at this late hour. He moves past a block of these and then another, moving in slow step with one arm folded around his middle to hold a rib he hopes is only bruised.

When in time he comes upon a light in a window it is the pink buzz of old neon spelling out a name. MABELS PIANO BAR.

A dented cowbell clangs above the doorway through which the piano player passes. The room he enters is cooled by a flow of pressing air. Faces cast in blue haze turn or they don't and those that do, finding nothing of interest, return numb gaze to drink or to thoughts hidden behind eyes unfocused. The piano player steps to the bar.

A barkeep watches a muted television. The bright colors of a game show. His beard and hair are sculpted with a fastidious care. When the piano player orders a drink there passes some seconds before the barkeep turns. His eyes widen and they settle again and he says okay. The piano player describes a drink and the barkeep again says okay and he pours a glass full, liquid the color of copper and a single cube of ice. The piano player sips and he pays the barkeep and sips again.

Beyond the bar there sits a piano painted a cool cream hue. One leg is shorter than the other, leaving the frame to lean on that end. The piano player with his one good eye looks on at the machine with its works and keys hidden away behind dust-covered wood.

The barkeep is again studying the TV screen when the piano player speaks.

"Is the owner around?"

"The owner never comes in," says the barkeep without turning.

A silent man on the screen is pointing at items while a man with a microphone stands at his side. The piano player goes on.

"Mabel?"

The barkeep turns up a smirk.

"There's no Mabel. That's just a name."

The piano player sits drinking a moment. Then he is up and with drink in one hand and ribs in another he is crossing the space between himself and the piano, and he sits, the bench's cushioned seat giving a gentle huff. He sips his drink and sets it in the gathered dust on piano top. Lid whines as keys are exposed. Old ivory is chipped in places, in places worn by the caress of fingers long ago forgotten. The piano player presses a key and a solid bong cuts through the room. He does this a second time, a third. Then he closes his eyes.

The song he plays is forlorn, melodic. Not quite in tune and not quite not. Something familiar to the gathered present but familiar in the way of smoky, half-remembered dream. Some listen and some go on with their talk and some only drink, and soon the piano player's song has ended.

He touches the lid and lowers it to once more hide away the world inside. He leaves that hand there atop the lid a moment, and then he is taking up his glass and drinking it down, he is standing, he's crossing back to the bar. He sits with that arm again holding his middle. He sets the glass on the bar and he points and he nods. The barkeep pours.

"Do you hire?"

"What?"

"Are you the one who does the hiring here?"

The barkeep nods.

"I can do that."

"Okay then. I'll play your piano. For tips and drinks."

He looks around the room.

"I'll give you half if I can sleep here."

"Hang on now."

The piano player puts out the hand not holding ribs. He says go on then. He says it'll be okay. The barkeep watches that hand hover and tremble as it waits, then he takes it, gives it a shake. The piano player nods.

"Okay."

The barkeep turns to patrons and to serving and he drifts away into the gloom. When he is gone a man in a silver suit rises from the bar and takes up a half-empty glass and an overlarge cowboy hat and he comes to sit by the piano player. He lays hat and glass down on bar top and he lets moments go by and then he says well. He says the barkeep is wrong. There was a Mabel. Her father ran the place during prohibition, a smalltime hood, dumb and mean. Mabel took it over in 1940-something.

The piano player takes a drink. The man in the silver suit asks if he can buy the piano player another.

"I pay for my drinks with song."

"Well then. You can buy me another."

The piano player drinks his drink. The other man introduces himself as a gambler and a historian. He says his grandfather knew Mabel way back.

"Was he a gambler too?"

"Not like that. He was the law in town."

He goes on. He says she was old by then, something of a real gangster, partnered with a Polish newspaperman who ran drugs and owned mayors. The gambler talks his way through histories arcane or fabricated whole cloth, and the barkeep brings more drinks, and faces shift and change in the dim, and when the piano player in time plays a song the gambler lays a generous tip on the bar and departs.

The barkeep's nose is bleeding. He enters the barroom empty of patrons, the pink neon lifeless and dark. The piano player taps his idle way through a half-realized tune and a bouncer at the bar is counting out stacks of currency and chewing on a pen and these men are alone in the room. The barkeep crosses the room in long steps and reaches across the bar and under and he comes up with a handful of ice. He lays this on a napkin and wraps it and presses the wrapped ice to his right hand. He lowers himself to a barstool seat.

The bouncer looks up from his count and he looks down again.

"Rough night?"

The barkeep blows out a long breath.

"I had a disagreement."

The bouncer lets out a snorting laugh. The piano player goes on playing his song as he turns to watch this scene. He watches and the barkeep turns his way and the piano player turns back to his song. The barkeep takes a bottle and pours a glass full and drinks. He sits a moment and then he reaches into a pocket and takes out a wallet. From this he pulls bills that he folds and puts back into the pocket. The wallet is tossed to land in a garbage can behind the bar. The bouncer looks up again.

"A disagreement?"

"Yeah, well."

The bouncer goes back to his count. The barkeep drinks his drink while the ice slowly melts on his hand. The piano player at bar's end goes on playing a halfhearted song.

It's some long hour of the night. It's an hour in a place between night and morning. The piano player plunks out a half-formed tune in a darkened, empty bar. He takes a hand from the keys and takes up his glass and drinks while the other hand goes on playing the loose idea of a song.

The thump of a bolt turned in its socket is loud in the room. The piano player turns to the door and turns back. Enter the barkeep. He stops when he hears the song, when he sees the piano player's back. His pause is only a moment, and then he is moving, he is crossing the room, rounding the bar. From under the bar he takes a zippered bag with the name of a bank stamped on its side. He presses a button on the bar's register and a bell chimes and the drawer opens with the jangle of coins splashing in its tray. He takes up bills and counts and separates them into three stacks on the bar.

The door opens. Enter the bouncer. He too pauses and stares at the piano player's back. He looks to the barkeep and the barkeep nods and the bouncer crosses the room.

A safe is opened and the count goes on. The two men talk of money and of the owner, and the piano player drinks and plays his song. He looks up when the bouncer takes one stack of bills and puts it in an envelope. He watches as the barkeep does the same. The barkeep meets the piano player's look and the piano player looks away. Each envelope is tucked away in a pocket, the bouncer's, the barkeep's, and the barkeep takes up the bank bag, and they cross the room, they leave the bar, the door's bolt snapped home once more, and alone the piano player sits in the empty barroom, drinking his drink, playing his song.

They come to the gambler at the bar. They speak a number or the name of a team, and he writes in a notebook, he writes out a ticket. Sometimes they bring money or some bauble of personal import to square a debt and he tips his overlarge cowboy hat and they go.

The piano player stands between songs. He brings an empty glass to the bar. He calls for a drink and the barkeep nods and goes on serving customers who pay with a more tangible currency. He turns to the gambler as he waits.

"Are you a criminal?"

The gambler laughs.

"That's a fine question."

"Well. What do you do?"

The gambler shifts on his stool. He looks up at the piano player. He says he makes people believe in a dream, and he says he makes book, and he says he is a criminal but that what he does is no crime. He says there are killers and wannabes and those somewhere in between, and though even those individuals may themselves not know which label best fits who they are, though even they may believe themselves something better or worse, all, when asked, will give an answer that is something less than a truth, and all will say more with their answer than the answer alone.

"Now," says the gambler to the piano player, "are you a criminal?"

The piano player shakes his head no. "I just play the piano."

The barkeep is watching the bouncer. The bouncer leans his head out the door and he turns one way and then the other. He looks back at the barkeep and shakes his head. A loose sprinkling of patrons mill about drinking watered drinks and coming and going. The piano player is playing his song. The bouncer leans out again. He stands watching the street. When he steps back into the barroom he nods once at the barkeep. The man who follows him in two steps behind is bone thin and small. Jeans and t-shirt hang loose on a string of a frame. He removes dark glasses and blinks twice. The bouncer points at the barkeep and the thin man heads that way. He stops and eyes bottles arrayed in their glittering rows but he does not order a drink. He lays hands on the bar and he says to the barkeep three days. He says the guy will be flush from the game, he won't have paid out yet. He says who knows how much they can take.

They go on talking, they go on planning. Some time has passed when the barkeep sees the piano player watching their talk. The barkeep stares back.

"What?"

The piano player takes a moment.

Then.

"I'm only here to witness."

The barkeep stiffens, he straightens.

"The fuck you just say to me?"

"Your business is your business, not any of mine."

The barkeep goes on watching the piano player. The thin man watches the barkeep. After some seconds they lean again to their talk.

His song ends when they burst through the door. The barkeep, the bouncer. The barkeep wears a duffel bag held to his body with a strap across his trunk. The bouncer's face is wet with sweat and splashed blood. Each man's arm ends in a gun.

The piano player turns on the bench.

The two men cross the barroom in long steps. They curse, they rant. The bouncer says we have to go back. The barkeep says we can't. The bouncer says we can't stay here. The barkeep says okay. He says just let me think.

The piano player watches.

The door is opened with a kick. The two are still turning when the bullets start to fly. The bouncer is struck six times and he slumps in a heap, and the barkeep is rolling across the bar, he is falling to the wood floor beyond. The gambler in his silver suit and overlarge cowboy hat stands waiting in the open doorway. After a dozen seconds he raises the gun and fires a round into the wall behind the bar. A hand comes up from the bar in response with gun firing back in all manner of direction before retreating again to obscurity. Another span of seconds falls away.

Then.

"I just want what's mine. You've no right to it."
And.

"That bar does nothing for you. I could shoot right through that wood."

"So could I."

Three pops spaced apart and aimed at nothing splinter bar front from behind. The gambler raises his weapon and fires once at the space between the newly made holes. A gasp comes back, and a hard thump. The gambler waits another moment and then he is crossing the empty space, he is leaning over the bar.

And here is where the piano player stands, and here is where he lurches his way through the barroom. When he steps into the night he leaves behind him Mabel's Piano Bar with its old wood and old stories and old violence. He moves with a hand at his middle where blood runs through fingers from a hole made by some bullet or other. He moves slow with eyes front, and when he arrives at a bench he does sit, waiting for the bus to ferry him to the next town.

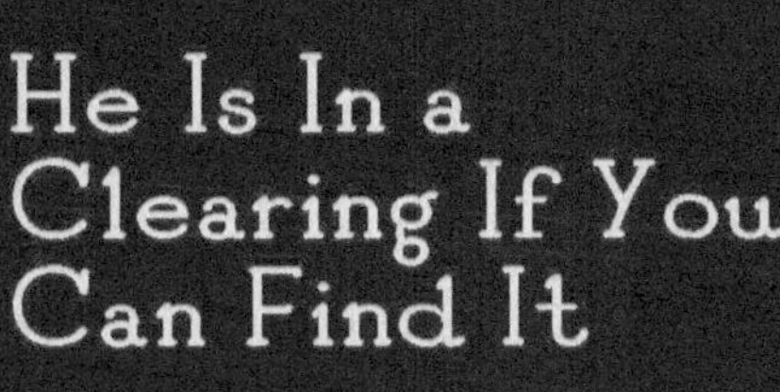

He Is In a
Clearing If You
Can Find It

He has a beer, she has a beer. It's a little thing, a garnish. A modest flirtation with teen rebellion. He took them from his mother's refrigerator. Now they sip at their beers, he does, she does, as they sit on a city bench waiting for her bus to come. They talk of the day they've had and of tomorrow and next week. They touch hands. They talk of imagined somedays and sip their beers. Sometimes they laugh. She asks about a memory they together share. He asks about her bus, if she wants to wait and take the next one. She asks about next time.

"We could go for a walk. In the woods, I mean. By the park."

"We could go see the man."

He laughs when he says it. She only stares. It takes him a minute. Then.

"You know. The man in the woods."

She shakes her head no.

"I don't understand."

He takes a deep drink. Bottle slosh glugs.

"It's just an old story. The older kids tell their brothers and sisters to scare them."

"That there's a man in the woods?"

"Well. They tell it a lot of ways."

He shifts on the bench. One foot tucks into the crook of the other leg's knee. He lays an arm across the benchback. Then he begins.

"They say he's in a clearing if you can find it. But there's no trail, just dense woods you go around like a maze and then there you are. Sometimes when they tell it the clearing moves around so no two people ever remember coming to it in quite the same place, and no one person can ever find it twice. They say he sits on a tree stump with a case on his lap. It's a case like a, like an old violin case. And if you give him a nickel he'll open up that case and play you a song."

Now she laughs a single, pure guffaw.

"You're making this up as you go."

His eyes widen, his mouth makes an O.

"I'm not!"

And.

"I swear I'm not. How have you never heard these?"

She takes a tiny sip from her bottle.

"Keep going."

And he does.

"Well. if you pay him a nickel he'll play you a song, but it's not always the same song for everybody. Sometimes it's a sad song, and sometimes it's."

He stops, he looks down, searching for a word.

"Jaunty. And how he chooses which depends on who's telling the story. Sometimes it's that he looks you up and down, and sometimes he leans in and gives your soul a sniff, and then sometimes there's no explanation at all, as if he's getting his guidance from some source beyond anything we could hope to understand."

"And then what?"

"And then. And then it depends on the song. If you get the happy one."

"Jaunty."

"Yeah. If you get the jaunty one you'll have all the good luck you can stand."

Her face contorts and she makes a noise like a snort.

"Come on."

"What?"

"Good luck? That's lame."

He shakes his head.

"Not if you believe in luck."

She looks at him. One finger taps at the bottle in her hand.

"Go on."

"Well there's also the sad song."

Her voice is softer now when she speaks.

"What happens if he plays the sad song?"

"Oh you wouldn't want to hear about that."

She slaps his arm. He laughs. She does it again.

"Finish the story!"

"It depends on who's telling. They all tell that part their own way. But every time. Every time. It's always something terrible."

A moment passes when she waits for something more, and then the bus is there, it is pulling to the curb, and she hands him her bottle, and he sets it down, and as they stand he dashes forward with a quick brush of lips against her cheek.

The bus doors open with a sigh. She steps in and turns to watch him go as the bus pulls away. When he is only a speck she makes her way up the aisle. She looks down at her feet with each step. Hands hold the backs of seats as she moves. Her smile beams. It hangs there a moment still when she looks up before a slow withering takes it away.

A long case is lain across his knees. He sits alone in the arrangement of seats. The curves of that timeworn trunk hint at the instrument held within. When she again moves she crosses the distance in wary steps. His old eyes come up to meet hers. Each clasp on that case pops open one by one with a satisfying thwap. When he lifts the lid with bent, skeletal fingers it gives a rending shriek like a thing sealed in antiquity. She holds out a nickel before her.

Going Home Again

att lays the handset in its cradle. He stands staring down where it lies a moment longer, as if it will ring again, as if something will be different. When he moves he moves out of the room and down the hall. He picks up keys from a table, and when he leaves he does not lock the door behind him. Again he pauses, thinking or pretending to, considering turning around, considering whether to decide none of this is real. Then he is moving, he is walking down steps and crossing the lot to a car, he is slumping into its seat. Here he sits, moments passing, not thinking now but not ready to let go and be carried away.

He turns the key.

He makes one stop, he wheels in at an ATM and takes out all the machine will allow, and then he is driving, he is getting on the highway headed west.

Thirty minutes of road go by when a figure appears on the median and grows near and in a blur is overtaken. Matt slows the car and he stops and sits looking in the mirror at the figure passed by. Seconds fall away. Then he is shifting gears, he is reversing, and the figure is there, a man, thin, flesh pale, a patched dusting of dark beard. Held in two hands is a torn scrap of cardboard on which is written a single word. ONWARD. The window comes down.

"Thanks for stopping."

"You okay?"

"Fine, fine."

"How far you got to go?"

"Not too far," says the thin man.

"Well. Come on, then."

The thin man pulls open the door and slides into the seat and with door closed the world again begins to move.

"So," Matt says to the thin man, and the thin man says oh, he says I'm going to a town up ahead a couple hours. He says as far as you can take me is fine. He says I can pay. Matt waves a hand at this and he says it's no trouble. There is quiet for a time and there is the white noise hum of tire on road and then the thin man speaks.

"What about you?"

"What?"

The thin man points at the road and the world and the way ahead.

"Where are you headed?"

For a moment the quiet is there again. For a moment the static drone of the onrushing present is the only sound. Then Matt smiles. Then he begins to speak.

"Home. A little fishing town on the coast."

"Oh yeah? You fish?"

"I don't. I never did. I'd go to the pier though. When I was a kid. There was this old man there every day. He'd lay this beat-up hat on a bench and when the boats came in he'd play tunes on an accordion. Just notes that bled one into another. And sometimes the fishermen would give him money, and sometimes they'd give him fish. And the tourists. The tourists would give him dollars to take a photo with him and his accordion. He'd have this big grin."

His talk trails off, and his smile in time begins to fade, and though the thin man responds and he talks for some time, Matt is far away, on a pier in some hazed long ago.

Full dark has come when he pulls into a motel lot. He brings with him no things and when he leaves the motel foyer with a room key he does not go to the room but crosses fifty yards of open macadam to a neon sign reading *BAR*. He enters and he sits and speaks the name of a drink, and when he pays he does so with cash, with a wad of bills he does not count. He sips and minutes pass and then a woman is sliding onto the stool at his side, in a smoky voice she is asking him what he's drinking. He says the name again, and in that same sultry hum she orders another for him and one for her. He pays again with cash, and as they are waiting she speaks.

"You on your way someplace?"

"I'm staying across the street tonight."

"Just tonight?"

He tells her yeah. He tells her he's on his way back to where he grew up, to a little fishing town. He tells her there was a man there when he was a kid, a smiling old man with an accordion who would play as the boats came in. He tells her something's happened and he has to go home.

She pats his leg, she smiles with gentle warmth. She makes an offer and he agrees to her terms. Their drinks come and they each drink them down and she follows him out to his room.

He swings his legs over the edge of the bed and puts feet on floor and standing nude he takes up pants from a chair where they lay and pulls bills from a pocket. He counts out what was agreed upon and he doubles it and this he leaves on a table by the door. She sits on the bed watching a quieted television and for the length of half a minute he is watching too without seeing the images there and then he is moving, he is rounding the bed and stepping into a bathroom painted the color of beach sand. He reaches into the shower and turns on the hot water. He sits on the side of the tub and with hands on knees he begins to weep. When he shuts the water off and steps back into the bedroom she has gone.

#

Through morning and midday miles of road cracked and meandering do pass under car as he heads ever west as if dragged onward by the passing sun. When he stops it is at a truck stop an hour from his journey's end. He fills up and goes in and pays at a counter at one end of a long room adorned with racks of cans and cookies and road necessaries. Beyond the aisles and racks there is a partition and on the other side are booths and tables and a length of old wood counter at which sit men drinking coffee, eating burgers and thick slabs of potato from baskets lined with papers checked in red and white.

Matt sits at the counter and orders a sandwich and as he waits a man steps near. The man says his name, he says Matt, the word ending in the lilt of interrogative. Matt says oh, he says hey. He does not say the man's name because he does not remember it, some collection of syllables whose relevance ceased in a long-ago move. Edwin, Edgar. Some Ed. This Ed asks Matt if he's heading back to town and Matt says yes, he says he is. He says he is going to go see the pier.

The man waits a beat, as if he is waiting for some next thought to come along and add to this last, but it does not. It does not.

"The pier?"

"You remember that old man there? With the accordion, when we were kids."

This Ed stares a moment more. He says well. He says it'll be good to be back home. He slaps a hand on Matt's back and he steps away and is gone.

#

The flooding pinks of dusk have come as he passes along empty streets on his way through town. The blinking red light of a four-way stop halts him midway. He sits there for a span of seconds, windows low, breathing a taste of air he'd forgotten he ever knew. Then he is again moving, navigating familiar roads until he comes to a vast and empty lot at the edge of the world. He gets out and he walks across those acres of pavement broken by time, lines faded and gone. When he reaches a rusting fence he passes through a section fallen to lie in wild grasses sprouting through fissured cement and here he stands under a pier roofed in black wood rotting away and in places broken off to lie in dust below. Ahead there is a bench and on it sits a dented hat and beside these there stands an old man smiling a great, wide smile, and in his old hands he holds an accordion.

Matt moves onward, he steps to the pier's end under dusk's splash of brilliant pink, and as he looks down at the world echoed on that lapping canvas of sea, a song begins to play.

King Bronislav

1. The Call

The room is set in dark. He does not see the bundle at first. Calvin Lond shuts the door and crosses to his desk and as he sits and leans to pull the string of one shined oxford it is here that his eye falls on the bundled paper in the corner. He pauses, he stares. Seconds go by. Then he is pulling the string of the second shoe and setting both oxfords alongside the desk and on stocking feet he pads back to where the paper lay. He bends and takes up the bundle and squatted there he turns it in his hands. He slides off three bands of elastic and unwraps the bundle and bills spill onto the floor. Twenties, fifties, hundreds. These he rakes together and with them piled on the sheet of paper he moves again to the desk.

A pull chain is tugged and a bare bulb pops on and yellow light spreads from a desk lamp. Calvin lays a hand alongside the money and with the other hand he pulls the paper from underneath. He holds the sheet up and reads it in the light.

ARE YOU A FINDER OF THINGS LOST?

These words written in a wild hand. Below this is a phone number. Calvin takes a phone from its cradle and dials the number and a voice comes on, a man speaking just above a whisper.

"Have you heard of the King Bronislav?"

"What is this?"

There is breathing and there is silence and there is nothing. Then that whisper of voice is there again, it is saying the King Bronislav is a violin crafted centuries ago and in the passing of years the violin has changed hands many times and until recently one such set of hands resided at 1223 Samuel Road.

"Why until recently?"

Silence again and that breathing as seconds go by.

Then.

"Call the number again when you've found it."

There is a click and the voice is gone, and as Calvin sets the handset back in its cradle he stares down at the note with its chaotic script and he contemplates tearing it up and forgetting this moment but instead he begins counting the money.

2. 1223 Samuel Road

He looks at a map as he drives. Housing divisions dot the countryside like primordial suburbs, satellites ejected from the city. Along a ridge he pulls to the side of the road. He takes a last look at the map before getting out of the long box of a car.

Below the ridge a valley of grassland runs for miles. Men in orange vests wander the valley like distant ants performing some arcane task while nearer there sits a single truck parked with the driver door open.

Calvin opens his back door. He gets in and removes his fine oxfords and unrolls socks and with bare feet on the grassy roadside he sits watching the men below go about their work. He reaches a hand up front and from the console takes a glass bottle sweating with fat droplets. He unscrews the cap and the bottle sighs and he drinks and goes on watching the distant figures. After some minutes, and when the bottle is empty of its drink, he rolls each sock back over its foot and he from the floor takes a pair of workboots worn, their leather in places thin and cracked. These he pulls on, and as he looks up from tying their laces he finds a foreman leaning from the below truck's open door and looking his way.

The hill pulls him down at a trot. On the valley floor he wades into grass and as he makes his way onward the foreman sits watching his approach. Some distance out he lifts a hand in wave and the foreman nods back and thirty seconds pass, forty seconds, and Calvin is there where the foreman sits unmoving in the truck doorway, as if he has been here waiting always.

"Hello there."

The foreman nods again and as Calvin nears there passes a moment where nothing happens and maybe nothing will and then Calvin is holding out a hand and the foreman is taking it and giving it one plain shake.

"Maybe you can help me."

"Maybe so."

The foreman's voice is a wet sound. A thick plug of tobacco leaves a bulge in his lip that bobs as he talks. He nods again at nothing in particular.

"I'm trying to find 1223 Samuel."

The foreman looks on a moment more and he gives another nod and reaches behind him to a tablet. He lays it in his lap and looks out at the open field for a throw of seconds before lighting up the tablet's screen and scrolling through first documents and then a satellite map. He looks out at the grassland and points.

"Walk say three hundred yards that way and you're dead on it."

Calvin does not turn around. A moment goes by in silence.

Then.

"What happened here?"

The foreman takes a styrofoam cup from the dash and looses a string of brown saliva into its depths.

"Flooded out. When the rains came through last year they opened up the spillway, but the mechanism was rotted out and they couldn't get it back shut. Condemned the whole valley. Demolished whatever was still here."

Now he does turn and he looks but there is nothing to see but the soft wave of grasses and here and there men moving about with their instruments. The foreman speaks.

"What's your business with it?"

"I'm looking for an item that was in that house. A musical instrument."

"Huh. It sure as shit isn't there now."

"Well," says Calvin, and, "Where did the debris end up?"

"County contracted somebody to haul it off."

The foreman puts up a finger. Wait. He reaches behind the seat into a pocket attached at its back and comes back with an aluminum clipboard thick with sheets of varied color and size. He flips pages up and lets a clump drop back into place and he does this two times more and then he is nodding, he is saying there we go.

"Eustace Doubleday."

"Eustace."

"Eustace Doubleday. He runs a scrapyard, but they contract out for all sorts of stuff."

He pulls the yellow slip from the clipboard and holds it up. One finger taps the page.

"Address."

Calvin's shift is barely a glance. The foreman holds the slip up a moment longer.

"Don't need to write it down?"

Calvin shakes his head no.

"Eustace Doubleday," he says.

3. *Eustace Doubleday*

The long car rolls slow on a worn path tight on each side with rows of rusting hulks of automobiles from all eras. They start with rusting art deco and progress through time as he comes on. Here and there the bulk of a piece of farm equipment stands out like some ambassador sent to mingle. After the last line of cars a fence topped with razor wire runs off in the distance each way. A gate stands open wide and the path leads onward to a series of sheds of varied sizes from closet to hangar and a single concrete building squat and simple like a garage with no house.

Calvin pulls to a stop at the concrete structure's back. There are no lined spaces but only ruts in the dirt left by visitors past. The engine ticks. He steps from the car into the drift of dust in the afternoon sun.

A thick door stands open in the concrete building. Calvin enters without knocking. A brief foyer stands bare and at its end is another open door. Somewhere an air conditioner chugs. Cool air wafts past Calvin and out into the day. He moves on.

Through the next door there is a cramped office, walls stacked with papers and boxes and the exposed innards of old electronics unrecognizable for the functions of their past lives. A desk takes up most of the room. A man sits at the desk facing the door, fine shirt with sleeves rolled to elbows, tie tucked between first and second button. His thinning hair is cropped and neat but with a wispiness that makes it baby fine. The junkman puts out a hand.

"Hello, Lond."

Calvin gives the hand a quick shake.

"Eustace."

Calvin sits in an open chair and lets hands rest on knees.

The junkman watches with the coy look of a smile only hinted.

"Has somebody hired you to come mess with my affairs again?"

Calvin sits back. His hands shift, fold in his lap.

"Not directly," he says.

Eustace's hinted-at smile materializes.

"Why have you come here?"

"I'm looking for an item."

"What luck. We've got a great many of those."

"I'm aware."

"Oh I know. That I do know."

An ancient, overlarge ashtray shaped like the hull of a ship sits at desk's edge, candies wrapped in colored plastics long since replacing ash. Calvin gestures a hand its way in unasked question.

"Please. Help yourself."

He takes three candies and slips two into a pocket. Plastic crinkles and he puts a piece of blue hard candy in his mouth where he moves it around a moment before tucking it in his cheek. The wrapper he folds twice and holds.

"Let me start with this. I don't care what you did."

"That so?"

"It is. I took this job more out of curiosity than anything."

"Okay."

"So. I'm looking for a violin."

"Uh huh."

The owner lived in the valley your guys cleared out last year. I know you. You don't let anything go by if it can make you money, and I know the bulk of that rubble didn't end up in any landfill. Tell me I'm wrong."

The junkman leans against the desk. He rests elbows with one hand folded in the other.

"Who hired you?"

"I don't know."

"You don't know."

"I do not."

"Exactly how is it an unknown someone has engaged your services?"

"There was an envelope in my apartment. In it was a stack of cash and a note with a phone number on it. I called it. The voice at the other end told me where to start."

The junkman stares across the desk. His smile has gone and now his face lies absent of any outward sign of his musing.

Then.

"Tell you what."

He pulls open a desk drawer and takes out a pad of stationary. From desktop he takes up a pen and scratches out words on pad and tears the top page from its moorings. He lays it on the desk with his hand on top.

"What this is, this is a riddle. I'll tell you where the violin went, but in exchange I want the answer to the riddle. However this comes out, I want to know who the voice on the phone is. Do we have a deal?"

"What if I don't find out who the voice is? What if the violin's sold and sold again and the trail's a dead end?"

"Then," says the junkman, " I guess that means you'll owe me?"

He slides the paper across the desk.

4. The Auctioneer

He takes one last look at the stationary in his hand.

BUNDY ELEMENTARY SCHOOL

and beneath that

AUCTIONEER

He crumples the page and tosses it into a wastebasket as he passes by. The hall goes on forever. Calvin's footsteps are loud slaps in the quiet. In time he comes to a counter where sits a brass door knocker. He stares. Somewhere crisp footsteps grow and fade without anyone appearing. He touches the knocker but the expansive quietude goes on. He raps knuckles on the dense countertop but no one comes. He waits. The footfalls come again and then a child rounds a distant corner and in her slow way approaches as if from miles out.

He stands watching this apparition as she nears, and when she comes to be some ten feet from Calvin she stops and only stares. He speaks.

"I'm looking for a man. An auctioneer."

His voice carries into the void.

"This is a school."

He nods and says nothing and she goes on staring.

"Excuse me."

He turns and at the counter there stands a woman of some twenty years with hair the white of blinding snow. She places both hands on the countertop and waits.

"Oh. I'm trying to find an auctioneer. I was told he works here."

She is nodding and she is saying yes, he works in the office.

"Is he around?"

"Go back outside and across the street. There's a shed and a building, looks like a big blue barn. You'll find him in there if he's here."

He thanks her and knocks once more on the countertop and he turns to offer some vague well wishing to the child but she has already gone. A bell begins to ring.

#

In the loft where once hay was stored there now sit filing cabinets and rows of bins marked with labels he cannot see from his vantage below. The ground floor is furnished with two desks and a table and enough chairs for a dozen souls but no one save Calvin is present. Off to the left there stands open a door and through this footfalls come and then not and a moment later they come again.

When Calvin steps through that gap he stands in a shed tall and long adorned with shelves reaching high and stacked with still more bins and naked machinery and other items unrecognizable to his experience. A warehouse of miscellany. Standing among these is a man in a suit the color of cream and a straw panama cocked back on his head. In his hands he holds a pen and overlarge notepad, and after a moment of reading a labeled bin with his face upturned he does write something in his notepad before moving on to the next.

"Hello?"

The man turns at the sound of Calvin's voice. An unlit cigarette hangs from his lip. He tucks the pen behind his ear and takes the cigarette from mouth with the same hand while the other drops the notepad on a shelf with an echoing slap.

"What's this then?"

"Are you the auctioneer?"

"That depends entirely on what you need with an auctioneer."

"I'm tracking down a violin."

The man blows air through pursed lips.

"Hoo. Well."

He gestures to the door at Calvin's back.

"Let's have us a seat and talk."

Calvin retreats to the makeshift office and drops into a chair facing the desk. The auctioneer follows him into the room.

"You drink?"

Calvin throws a glance at a clock on the wall. The hands read three oh seven.

"Sure thing," he says.

The auctioneer takes from a cabinet two glasses and a clear bottle with no label. He pours three fingers in each glass and sets the bottle on the desk and he lowers himself with ginger care into the seat nearest Calvin. He passes over one glass and holds the other in the same hand as the unlit cigarette and he nods and drinks. Calvin holds the glass, resting it on his thigh. The auctioneer drinks again and again exhales through pursed lips and he speaks.

"The King. Do you know about it?"

"A little."

The auctioneer takes the panama from his head and lays it on the desk.

"Well. From what I can tell it's sitting in an evidence lockup, waiting for the guy to go to trial."

Calvin's face does not visibly change but there is a shift, a stiffening felt more than seen. He sits and he raises the glass and sips and lowers it again.

"What?"

The auctioneer takes up the bottle and adds two fingers to his own glass.

"I bought it to sell. I didn't know about its history until later. I certainly didn't know who it belonged to."

"Who did it belong to?"

"Well nobody now. Some kid broke into my shop and took off with it."

"What kid? Do you have a name? Is he in county?"

Liquor sloshes from glass as the auctioneer shakes his head.

"Not county. He's in the town jail while they're sorting it out. Or he was. They didn't have a name on him. It's a damn thing."

"What does that mean, no name on him?"

"No ID on him, wouldn't own up to him having one. Nothing in the system on his prints. It made the paper."

"And he's in the town jail?"

"Last I heard."

Calvin's eyes are staring hard at some thought he does not share. The auctioneer upends his glass into his waiting maw. He points with the glass hand at the one Calvin still holds.

"Drink your drink," he says.

5. *Officer Lawton*

He is led through a corridor tiled in gray at whose end a steel door is opened to his approach. The officer steps through and Calvin steps through and the officer pushes shut the door. The coming clang is deep and dense and a hard click of a mechanism turning to lock does follow.

Barred cubicles line the room. A figure lies unmoving on a cot in one and a man in a fine suit with letters stamped on the knuckles of each hand reads a paper in another and other than these the cubicles sit vacant.

The officer points at the man lying on the cot. Calvin looks at the unmoving man and at the cop and again at the man. He steps nearer the bars.

"You stole something I'm looking for."

There is quiet and there is nothing and for a long moment it is so, and then comes a deep inhale, exhale. The man on the cot rolls slow and puts bare feet on the gray tile and stands. Unfurled, his form comes to five feet, his small frame wired with muscle. He looks out of eyes the same color as the floor.

"Hello," he says.

Calvin waits for more but there is no more.

"I've been following a violin. You're the last one to have it."

The man does not move, does not speak. His pose is loose, at ease. A man with no concerns.

"Do they have it locked up?"

Nothing.

"Why that item? Did someone hire you to steal it?"

Nothing.

"Do you know the voice on the phone?"

The small man's visage shifts now, and slowly he begins to smile. Then he is turning, he is moving to lie on his cot once more.

Calvin watches and he wants to speak but there is nothing left to say. He finds himself going back the way he came, the officer just ahead. After the steel door and after the gray hall comes an open foyer populated by shrugging houseplants and a front desk. Here the officer stops.

"Hang on."

He steps to the front desk and says something to an elderly man sitting there and then he is moving to the front door, he is gesturing for Calvin to follow.

Cool morning breeze skims flesh. Calvin pulls at his coat. The officer takes from pocket a square of plastic and raises it to his lips and breathes. He lowers it and blows vapor into the day.

"Look. Your violin's not in lockup."

Calvin stares.

"Okay."

"I don't know who got it out but it's a goddamn mess."

He puts the square of plastic to his face again. Blue vapor leaks as he talks.

"Last night we get a call, the guy it was stolen from, works for the school. He goes to meet a guy says he has the thing, wants to return it to the rightful owner, only when the school guy shows there's a body and no violin."

"A body."

The officer nods.

"Shot dead."

"Who was it?"

"Some roughneck. Local. We knew him."

"Where was the meeting?"

"Parking lot. No cameras. If anybody saw anything they didn't stick around."

"What did the auctioneer have to say?"

"Who?"

"School guy."

"Oh. Shaken up. He said the thing didn't even belong to him and nobody needed to be getting hurt over some shit like that."

"Okay. What about the dead guy? How did he contact the auctioneer? Did he know him?"

"Didn't know him. Guy said he got a phone call, out of the blue."

A moment goes by. Then.

"What did he say about the phone call?"

"Just said he got a phone call."

"And now the thing's just gone."

"Looks like," says the cop in a huff of pale blue.

6. The King Bronislav

The rusted clunk of the mail slot opening and closing is a slap in the quiet of the room. Calvin looks up to see a pale slip hit the floor. He crosses the room in three long steps. Eye to peephole but the courier has already gone. He stoops, he grabs. What he comes up with is a calligraphed work of some fine make, an ornate note with a simple message. *You are cordially invited to a night of dance and song.* The invite is for a hovel of a bar at the edge of town. There is no postmark.

A thick haze swirls as he opens the door. The room stinks of cigarettes and sweat. The floor is crowded with people and their noise. Calvin works his way between hot bodies to a bar lined with much of the same. He calls out the name of a spirit and the bartender says okay and he pours a glass high with clear liquid. Calvin sips and looks around but all there is to see is the mass of flesh writhing in the fume.

A man at his side turns to him with wet eyes rimmed in maroon. He breathes words.

"What are you drinking?"

The man's suit is the thick cloth of a cut long years out of fashion. He does not wait for an answer but only turns to the bartender and orders another and one for himself. A new glass is set next to the one Calvin has not touched. Where the stranger's glass is placed there sits a pack of cigarettes and a lighter etched with letters and symbols of ambiguous implication.

"Is that yours?"

The stranger says it is.

"As much as anything can ever be anyone's."

"What does that mean?"

"It used to belong to someone else, now it's mine."

Somewhere in the crowd a single fiddler begins to play. Calvin turns but the figure is lost in the swaying body and veil. Somber notes fill every empty space with their weighted poise. The stranger shakes a cigarette from the pack and sets it alight, filling the room with still more haze. Calvin drinks his drink.

Our Featured Performer

The lights are the world. Beyond their gleam there is ruffling and now and then a clearing of throat and there is a darkness, but on the stage the lights are all there is. Blinding and burning and throwing pale shine upon the man standing there.

He whispers his thanks to the gathered. His voice cracks and he says it again. From the crowd there is only quiet and the barest testimony of their continued residence exposed by their passive stirring. Smoke drifts in lazy swirls under the lights but the glow of cigarette somewhere in the crowd is burned away in the harsh throw of the overhead spots.

The man on stage lifts his instrument, a banjo stained with age. This man is the player, he is the performer. He takes a step nearer stage's edge and he squints into the light. He nods once. Then he begins to play.

The notes form a somber tune, slow, wistful. They rise and they fall and they pull at something lost, they take hold and they pull and don't let go and he goes on playing, sweating under the lights, beads forming on lip, running down ribs. His hands work the strings on their own and his mind is far away, lost in the song and in a feeling held there. He thinks he was a good man. He thinks he led a good life.

He stands alone on the stage as the sole architect of this hymn but the space between the notes is not bare. There exists a hum, or not a hum but an energy, a tone more felt than heard. Perspiration shows in damp patches on his buttondown. His eyes stare up into the lights.

His playing grows faster. The spots begin to dim but the heat is somehow worse as the song becomes angry, becomes bitter. There is a murmur or moan from the crowd but he cannot see them from his place on the stage. His fingers hurt but still he plays. The details of memory fade but he is sure he was a good man, he is sure he led a good life.

He's playing fast now, raging and desperate. The lights are gone and all is darkness. The crowd is screaming, shrieking. The performer is weeping, his fingers are bleeding. He plays his song tonight as he plays it every night. He thinks he was a good man. He thinks he led a good life.

About the Author

Craig Rodgers has an extensive collection of literary rejections folded into the shape of cranes and spends his time writing in North Texas.

Also by Craig Rodgers

The Ghost of Mile 43

Doing Time

Moonbeams

Twenty Ponds

Visitor

The End

www.ingramcontent.com/pod-product-compliance
Lightning Source LLC
Chambersburg PA
CBHW032010120726
47902CB00014B/2051